© 1995 Geddes & Grosset Ltd
Published by Geddes & Grosset Ltd,
New Lanark, Scotland.

ISBN  1 85534 559 5

Printed and bound in Great Britain.

# The Tin Soldier

Retold by Judy Hamilton
Illustrated by Lindsay Duff

## Tarantula Books

Once upon a time long ago, a little boy was given a box of tin soldiers as a birthday present. He opened the box and saw that there were twenty-five soldiers inside, all lying smartly in a row. They were beautifully painted, with bright red jackets and navy-blue trousers, each one a work of art. The little boy began to take the soldiers out of the box one by one and stand them to attention to show the other children. But when he took the last soldier out, he found that one of its legs was missing. What a disappointment!

But the little tin soldier could still stand as straight as any of the others and looked every bit as smart and proud.

The little tin soldier stood on the table and looked around. There were many toys to look at, but what caught his eye was a beautiful castle, made from paper. It was perfect in every detail, with a mirror for a lake in front of it. On the lake were tiny model swans, and around it were trees. But best of all was the beautiful ballerina paper doll which stood at the door of the castle. She wore a white floating dress and a blue sash over her shoulder with a sparkling stone in the middle of it. She had her arms outstretched and stood on one leg with the other kicked up high behind her. The tin soldier could not see her other leg at all.

"She is one-legged, just like me!" he thought, and fell in love with her there and then.

The tin soldier wanted to get to know the paper ballerina, but was not sure whether she would be interested in a humble soldier such as he.

"I have to share a cardboard box with twenty-four other soldiers, while she has that beautiful castle all to herself," he thought.

Still, he did not give up hope. He lay down behind a box on the table where he could still see the ballerina. When the rest of the soldiers were put away in their box that night, the one legged-soldier was left out. He stayed where he was, watching his beloved paper doll.

The toys all came to life that night, dancing and playing around the room and making a terrible racket. The soldiers in the box rattled and shook, cross because they could not get the lid off to get out to play. But the one-legged soldier stood to attention and gazed lovingly at the paper ballerina. The other toys danced and jumped all around her, but she stood as still as the tin soldier, perfectly balanced on one leg.

Suddenly the lid of the box flew open and out jumped a Jack-in-the-box. He saw the tin soldier watching the ballerina and became very angry.

" Stop staring, tin soldier!" he shouted, but the tin soldier payed no attention.

"Just you wait until tomorrow!" said the Jack-in-the-box.

Sure enough, the next morning, when the little boy stood the tin soldier on the window-sill, the window flew open as if by magic. The tin soldier fell down three storeys to the pavement below, landing with his head stuck between the paving-stones. The little boy came out to look for him, and the tin soldier wanted to call out, "Here I am," but he did not think that it was the proper thing for a soldier in uniform to do. It began to rain and the little boy gave up searching and went back inside.

The rain poured down upon the tin soldier. He stayed stuck there between the paving-stones until the rain stopped, when some other boys came along and spotted him.

"Look, a tin soldier!" said one. "Let's send him sailing down the gutter!"

The little boys found some newspaper and made a boat for the tin soldier. They picked him up and put him in the boat, then they set the boat down in the rain-filled gutter. The water was flowing fast, and the boat was carried along with the current, tossing from side to side. The boys ran down the pavement, clapping and cheering. The tin soldier began to feel quite sea-sick as the boat was thrown about in the water, but he kept himself firmly to attention, his rifle on his shoulder. The boat sailed on down the gutter until it came to a drain. Down it went with the tin soldier still inside, into the sewer below, dark and frightening.

"That Jack-in the-box has done for me, for sure," thought the tin soldier. "If only my beloved ballerina doll was with me. Then I would not care what happened."

Just then a great water rat stepped in front of the boat.

"What are you doing here?" demanded the rat, baring its yellow teeth. "Have you got a passport?"

The tin soldier remained at attention and did not reply. The boat sailed on, with the rat chasing behind, calling out,

"Stop, stop! Show me your passport!"

The water flowed even faster and the soldier could hear a roaring sound, getting louder and louder. They were reaching the place where the sewer flowed out into a canal. No matter how frightened he felt, the tin soldier never moved as he lay in the newspaper boat. He kept himself straight with his rifle at his shoulder.

"Whoosh!" The water spilled out of the sewer pipe and down into the canal. The tin soldier was swept right down the waterfall and landed with a splash in the canal. The paper boat filled up with water and began to sink. Stiff and straight as ever, the tin soldier felt himself going down in the murky waters. He thought of his pretty paper ballerina and realised he was probably never going to see her again. He thought he was going to die. The waterlogged newspaper boat went to pieces and the tin soldier fell through.

At that very moment a great big fish swam up. It snatched the tin soldier up in its mouth and swallowed him whole.

It was dark and cramped in the stomach of the fish, but the tin soldier remained as staunch as ever, lying full length, still shouldering his rifle. He could feel the fish twisting and turning violently as it swam. It was even worse than being in the paper boat in the gutter. Then all of a sudden the fish was still.

The tin soldier did not know what was happening. He lay there, absolutely still in the blackness, for a long time. The next thing he saw was a flash of steel and then daylight streamed down upon him. The fish had been caught and taken to market, where it had been sold. And now it was in the kitchen and the cook was cutting it up and preparing it for dinner.

"Look! A tin soldier!" exclaimed the cook, and she took him out of the fish to clean him up.

The tin soldier was washed and then taken into the parlour. Everybody was interested to see what the cook had found inside the fish. What a strange journey for a toy to go on!

The tin soldier had been through such an ordeal that he thought that nothing could surprise him. He concentrated on keeping himself straight and proper, always to attention as a soldier should be. He was taken from the cook's hand and set to stand on the table.

It was then that the tin soldier realised that he had found himself back in the very same house as before, with the same children and the same toys. What luck!

The tin soldier was overjoyed to see the paper ballerina still in her place at the door of the paper castle. She stood unwavering on one leg, as steadfast as he had been. The soldier could have cried with happiness, but that would not be a proper thing for a soldier to do. So he simply gazed at the paper ballerina with his heart full of love, and she gazed back at him.

But the Jack-in-the-box was not finished with the tin soldier. He still had evil to work. And so it was that one small boy suddenly picked up the tin soldier, and without any reason, threw him into the fire. The heat was terrible; but the tin soldier kept his eyes on the ballerina. Scraped and battered after his journey, he remained as brave as ever.

Was it the fire or his love for the ballerina which caused such a heat? The tin soldier did not know. But he could feel himself begin to melt as he stood there, watching his beloved paper doll.

Then a door was opened in the room and a draught blew in. It caught up the paper ballerina and swept her into the fire beside the tin soldier. She burst into flames and disappeared, just as the tin soldier melted.

Next morning when the maid was cleaning out the fire, she found that the tin soldier had melted right down. All that was left was a lump of tin in the shape of a heart. And all that remained of the paper ballerina was the sparkling stone from the middle of her sash, blackened with soot.